This toddler talkabout
belongs to

Using this book

Ladybird's toddler talkabouts are ideal for
encouraging children to talk about what they see.
Bold, colourful pictures and simple questions help
to develop early learning skills – such as matching,
counting and detailed observation.

Look at this book together. First talk about the
pictures yourself, and point out things to look at.
Let your child take her* time. With encouragement,
she will start to join in, talking about the familiar
things in the pictures. Help her to count objects,
to look for things that match, and to talk about
what is going on in the picture stories.

*To avoid the clumsy use of he/she, the child is referred to as 'she'.
Toddler talkabouts are suitable for both boys and girls.*

Acknowledgement:
Cover illustration by Terry Burton

Published by Ladybird Books Ltd
80 Strand London WC2R 0RL
A Penguin Company
9 10 8

© LADYBIRD BOOKS LTD MCMXCVIII

Printed in Italy

I like
farm
animals

illustrated by Richard Morgan
and Andy Everitt-Stewart

Ladybird

Who lives on the farm?

What animal noises can you make?

What is happening in this story?

What baby animals can you see?

How many lambs can you count in each box?

Match these animals with their homes.

Can you match the animal to its blue shadow?

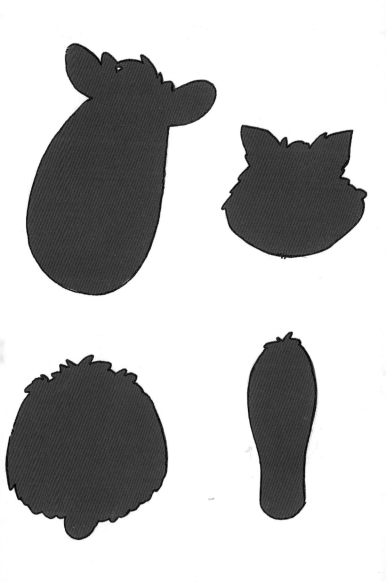

Say what is happening in each box.

Find another...

cow

duck

horse

Which is your favourite
farm animal?

What are the goats doing in this story?

Sing 'Old Macdonald had a farm...'